Junior Seau

Junior Seau

Star Linebacker

Jeff Savage

Enslow Publishers, Inc.

44 Fadem Road	PO Box 38
Box 699	Aldershot
Springfield, NJ 07081	Hants GU12 6BP
USA	UK

Library of Congress Cataloging-in-Publication Data

Savage, Jeff, 1961–
     Junior Seau : star linebacker / Jeff Savage.
        p. cm. — (Sports reports)
     Includes bibliographical references (p.   ) and index.
     Summary: Profiles the personal life and football career of the hard-working
linebacker for the San Diego Chargers.
     ISBN 0-89490-800-6
     1. Seau, Junior, 1969– —Juvenile literature. 2. Football players—United
States—Biography—Juvenile literature. 3. San Diego Chargers (Football team)—
Juvenile literature. [1. Seau, Junior, 1969– . 2. Football players. 3. Samoan
Americans—Biography.] I. Title. II. Series.
GV939.S393S28 1997
796.332′64′092—dc20
[B]   96-21532

Printed in the United States of America

10 9 8 7 6 5 4 3 2

To Our Readers:
All Internet addresses in this book were active and appropriate when we went to
press. Any comments or suggestions can be sent by e-mail to Comments@enslow.com
or to the address on the back cover.

Illustration Credits: Rich Pecjak, pp. 9, 18, 20, 27, 33, 42, 45, 63, 73, 74, 79, 82, 85, 88;
University of Southern California, pp. 49, 52, 59.

Cover Photo: Rich Pecjak

Contents

Chapter 1

AFC Champs

Barry Foster took the handoff. He ran straight up the middle. He was about to break free, when—*Boom!*—he was knocked off his feet by a crunching hit. San Diego Chargers linebacker Junior Seau had drilled the Pittsburgh running back to the turf. It was the first play of the game, and Junior was making a statement. His last name is pronounced SAY-OW. He was showing the Steelers they were in for a painful afternoon.

It was the 1995 AFC Championship Game at Three Rivers Stadium in Pittsburgh. The winner would go to the Super Bowl. Over sixty-one thousand fans were cheering for the Steelers and waving their yellow Terrible Towels. Everyone figured the Steelers would win the game. Pittsburgh defensive end Ray Seals predicted that the Chargers would not score a point. Four days before the game, the Steelers began making a Super Bowl rap video they would sell during Super Bowl week. Nobody gave the Chargers a chance. Nobody, that is, except the Chargers themselves.

Yancy Thigpen caught a 7-yard pass from Neil O'Donnell; then Foster ran for 7 more yards, and the Steelers had reached midfield. A light rain was falling. The field was slick as ice. Junior yelled for the Chargers to dig in.

Foster took a handoff and headed right. Seau blasted through one blocker, hurdled another, and smacked Foster to the ground. Junior didn't care that the Steelers had the NFL's top running game. He didn't care that they rushed for 238 yards the previous week in a playoff carving of the Cleveland Browns. He didn't even care that his own left arm was almost useless because of a midseason shoulder injury. Junior's job was to stop the run. That was what he intended to do. The only way Pittsburgh would move the ball was through the air.

A 9-yard pass to Ernie Mills got the Steelers another first down. Foster took a handoff and started left. Seau broke through the line and hammered the running back for a 3-yard loss. Junior jumped to his feet, let out a yell, and punched the air with his

Rising high above the pile, Junior Seau tries to throw his opponent for a loss.

right fist. It was his famous celebration dance, the Bolt. The crowd booed.

The Steelers tried a screen play. Foster took the pass and turned upfield. Just then, Seau came flying in like a guided missile. Foster was knocked backward for another loss. Junior pumped his arm and hopped—the Bolt again. The crowd booed even louder.

"That's why he's regarded as the best middle linebacker in the game," yelled television announcer Dick Enberg. "He's stunning!"[1]

The San Diego secondary couldn't stop the pass, however. Andre Hastings caught one pass for 18 yards and another for 11 to give Pittsburgh a first down at the 21. On the next pass play, Seau tried to help by blitzing. O'Donnell dumped a short pass to John L. Williams, who scooted clear to the end zone for a touchdown. The extra point gave Pittsburgh an early 7–0 lead.

The Chargers were quiet. Junior did not get upset with them. On the sideline, he told them to work harder. They saw the intensity in his eyes.

"[Junior] was quiet before the game, just sitting in [the locker room] and waiting, and then, when the game started, he exploded," said safety Stanley Richard. "Seeing him, you told yourself, I need to get out and start playing, because he's stepping up."[2]

Seau's determination inspired his teammates. The Steelers would not score another touchdown in the game.

Meanwhile, San Diego could barely move the ball on offense. Quarterback Stan Humphries was pressured by blitzing linebackers Greg Lloyd and Kevin Greene. Running back Natrone Means was swarmed by Pittsburgh's physical defense. Midway through the second quarter, the Steelers had out-gained the Chargers in yards, 165–16.

The Chargers awakened on their last possession of the half. First, Means powered over right tackle for 17 yards. Next, he took a swing pass down the right sideline for 15 more. Finally, wide receiver Shawn Jefferson beat cornerback Deon Figures on a bomb. Figures saved a likely touchdown by grabbing Jefferson's arm just before the pass arrived. The interference call placed the ball at the one-yard line. Could the Chargers tie the game?

On first down, Means took a handoff over right guard. No gain. On second down, Means tried the left side. No gain. On third down, he tried the middle. No gain. Means could not crack through the Steel Curtain. The Chargers settled for a field goal by John Carney, making the score 7–3.

FACT

Before Junior joined the NFL, people didn't know how to pronounce his last name (it's SAY-OW!). Even draft expert Mel Kiper called him Junior Say-OWL. Who? When the Chargers introduced Junior at the press conference on draft day, they said, "And here he is. . . . Junior So." But Junior got even. He thanked owner Alex Spanos by calling him "Span-YOz."[3]

The Steelers answered before the half. O'Donnell moved the ball through the air once again with passes down the middle to Mills, Hastings, Thigpen, and huge tight end Eric Green. Pittsburgh reached San Diego's 22-yard line with eighteen seconds left. The Steelers tried an inside handoff to Williams. Junior sniffed out the play. He lowered his shoulder—his injured left shoulder—and drove it into Williams. Seau stopped Williams for no gain, but Junior paid a heavy price. He crumpled to the ground in pain as Pittsburgh called time-out. Junior managed to get to the sideline, where he collapsed to the ground again. He didn't see Gary Anderson's kick sail through the uprights for a field goal. The Steelers led 10–3 at the half, but Junior Seau's courage had become the big story.

Most experts picked the Chargers to finish last in their division, the AFC West, but San Diego surprised everyone by beating out the Broncos, Raiders, Chiefs, and Seahawks to win the division and gain a playoff berth. Still, not many people believed the Chargers could beat Dan Marino and the Miami Dolphins in the first round of the playoffs. Junior Seau believed. "Ever since I was a kid I dreamed of going to the Super Bowl," said Junior. "That is the ultimate feeling of success. . . . We could be a team of destiny. We have a long way to go, but we could be."[4]

In their game against the Dolphins, the Chargers trailed 21–6 at halftime, and their season appeared over. Then Seau led a defensive charge that held Miami scoreless in the second half, and San Diego won by a point. It was the seventh come-from-behind victory by San Diego that season.

Could the Chargers do it again? In Pittsburgh? In the AFC title game? In the rain?

The second half did not begin well for San Diego. Humphries had completed just one pass in the first half. He was frustrated. On the third play of the third quarter, the San Diego quarterback tried to force the ball to a wide receiver. All-Pro cornerback Rod Woodson stepped up to intercept the pass near midfield.

The San Diego defense had to respond. It was no time to panic, but the Chargers already trailed by seven points and were having trouble scoring. They couldn't afford to get too far behind. On Pittsburgh's first play, running back Bam Morris was stopped for no gain. On second down, though, tight end Green got free behind linebacker Dennis Gibson and caught a perfect pass for 34 yards.

Seau was angry now. He yelled at Gibson to concentrate. On the next play, Junior blitzed and nearly stole the handoff from O'Donnell to Foster. As it was, he ran past the play, turned around, ran back the other way, and chased Foster down from behind. It was an amazing display of hustle and desire. "He never gives up!" shouted television commentator Bob Trumpy.[5]

Two plays later, a catch by Thigpen over the middle, and a face mask penalty against cornerback Dwayne Harper, put the ball at the San Diego 5-yard line. A touchdown would probably spell doom for the Chargers. On first and goal, Foster was stopped for no gain. On second down, Seau blitzed and forced O'Donnell to throw the ball away. On third down, O'Donnell overthrew his receiver. The Steelers had to settle for another field goal. With ten minutes left in the third quarter, Pittsburgh led, 13–3.

Then lightning struck. Andre Coleman returned the kickoff to the 35-yard line. Means blasted for 6 yards. Shawn Jefferson caught an 11-yard pass. From the Pittsburgh 43, the Chargers pulled off a great play. Humphries faked a handoff to Means. Steelers safety Carnell Lake bit on the fake. Tight end Alfred Pupunu ran past Lake. Humphries threw the ball to Pupunu, who was wide open at the 20. Pupunu caught the pass and outraced the Pittsburgh defenders to the end zone. The San Diego sideline erupted. Junior was one of the first players to greet Pupunu in the end zone. Seau and Pupunu are roommates for road games.

Carney kicked the extra point. The Chargers had cut the lead to 13–10. Was Junior Seau right? Could the Chargers be a team of destiny?

The teams traded punts. The third quarter ended. The teams traded punts again. The rain fell harder. The game grew tense.

With twelve minutes left, the Steelers took possession at their 19. Bam Morris tried the right side. Seau stopped him for no gain. Morris went left with another handoff. Seau ran him down from behind for no gain. Junior's left arm hung uselessly now, but still he made the plays with his good right arm. On third and long, O'Donnell hit Mills over the middle for 18 yards and a first down. The Chargers had to make a stop. They had to get the ball back. Seau took matters into his own hands. First, he blitzed O'Donnell into throwing an errant pass. Next, he chased down Foster on a swing pass and pulled him down with his right arm. Finally, he teamed with safety Darren Carrington in tipping away a pass across the middle. The Steelers were forced to punt.

Less than ten minutes remained. The Chargers took possession at their 20. After Levon Kirkland stuffed Means for no gain on first down, the Chargers called another play for Pupunu. Greg

Lloyd blitzed. Humphries got the pass away just in time. Pupunu was wide open again, and took the pass 24 yards to the 44. The Chargers called the same play in the huddle. It worked again. Pupunu gained 8 more yards. Junior Seau watched excitedly from the sideline. He had never seen his roommate so intense.

The Chargers reached Pittsburgh's 38-yard line with six minutes left. It was third down and nine. Three Rivers Stadium was blaring with noise and swirling with towels. It was so loud that Chargers tackle Harry Swayne couldn't hear Humphries's signals and committed a false start. Now, it was third and fourteen. The ball was at the 43. At the snap, Kevin Greene blitzed. Greg Lloyd blitzed. Chad Brown blitzed. Humphries stood tough. He threw deep, then got clobbered. The ball arched toward the end zone. Wide receiver Tony Martin was running a fly pattern. He had cornerback Tim McKyer beaten by a step. The ball came down perfectly. Martin leaped and caught it going into the end zone. The Chargers had taken the lead. Carney's extra point made it 17–13 with five minutes left.

Now it was up to the defense. O'Donnell had riddled the secondary all day. He would set AFC Championship Game records for most passes attempted and completed, and he would move the

Steelers downfield again. Tight end Green caught a pass for 17 yards. Williams gained 7 more over the middle before Seau could wrap him up. There were four minutes left, and the clock was ticking.

Mills caught a pass across midfield in front of Darrien Gordon for 13 yards. Williams caught a swing pass for 4 yards, but Seau kept him in bounds. Three minutes were left. Tick. Tick. Tick.

Williams took a screen pass 3 yards. Green slipped behind linebacker Gibson to catch another pass for 8 yards to the 30. Tick. Tick. Tick. Then Green raced past Gibson again, and O'Donnell threw a perfect strike. The big tight end rumbled with the ball down to the 9. "C'mon!" Seau yelled at Gibson. The clock stopped at the two-minute warning.

The season had reached the brink. The Steelers needed a touchdown. They had to go 9 yards. They had four downs to do it. Everyone expected them to score. No one expected a defensive stand. Not now. A San Diego victory would be the biggest upset in AFC Championship Game history. It couldn't happen, could it?

On first down, the Steelers ran a draw play. Foster went left. Defensive end Leslie O'Neal slowed him up. Defensive tackle John Parella grabbed his legs. Junior Seau finished off the tackle.

Seau is shown here talking to a fellow teammate. Seau is more than just a star player, he is also the leader of the San Diego Chargers' defense.

On second down, O'Donnell threw short over the middle to Green. Gibson and Seau reached together to bat the ball away.

On third down, Williams caught a slant-in across the middle. Seau grabbed him from behind at the 3-yard line and held on. Linebacker David Griggs jumped in to help, but it was Seau who saved the touchdown.

It all came down to one play. Fourth down. Three yards to go. One minute left. The Steelers called time-out. The Chargers discussed defensive strategy on the field. Junior told his linebacker mates to jump in front of receivers if they could. In the huddle, Junior called for a defense called the Picket Fence.

O'Donnell took the snap and dropped back to pass. He looked for Green. Junior Seau had him covered. O'Donnell was forced to look elsewhere. He spotted Foster at the goal line. He threw hard and low. Foster crouched to make the catch. Dennis Gibson came flying forward. Gibson jumped in front of Foster at the last instant and batted the ball away with his left hand. The ball hit the turf, incomplete. The Chargers had won it! They poured onto the field in a wild celebration. The Terrible Towels stopped twirling. The crowd was stunned.

Three Humphries snaps and kneel-downs, and it was over. The San Diego Chargers were headed to

Seau remains focused at all times. Seau led the Chargers to the 1995 Super Bowl by making 16 tackles in the AFC championship game despite playing with a badly injured left shoulder.

their first-ever Super Bowl. They had Junior Seau to thank for it. He finished the game with 16 tackles and countless inspirational moments. He had come to Pittsburgh to make a statement. In doing so, he carried his team to a stunning victory.

In the locker room, Junior was still focused and intense. "You can never measure character," he told reporters. "You can never measure heart. You saw it out there today. You don't know whether to cry, to laugh, to smile. This is a great moment for San Diego and for everyone in the organization. That's how big this is."[6]

Afterward, Seau dressed, kissed his wife, and walked silently to the team bus. All around him, players stopped to hug friends and family members, and to sign autographs for fans. Not Junior. He walked directly to the bus, saying nothing. His actions said everything.

FACT

Offensive players usually get the glory in the NFL. Only two defensive stars since 1970 have been named the league's Most Valuable Player, awarded by the Associated Press. They were Minnesota Vikings defensive end Alan Page, in 1972, and New York Giants linebacker Lawrence Taylor, in 1986. Junior has his sights set on becoming the third. "I want to be the most valuable player in the whole league," he says.[7]

Chapter 2

Early Life

Junior Seau grew up in a garage. His family was poor and could not afford a house with enough bedrooms for all six children, so Junior shared the one-car garage with his older brothers. The concrete floor was cold. The roof leaked. Junior slept each night in the right corner by the door, between an old dishwasher and a box of cleaning supplies. "We thought everyone slept in the garage," he said. "We didn't know any different."[1]

Junior's family had moved to the United States when Junior was five. They came from American Samoa, a group of islands in the South Pacific. Junior could not speak any English; nor could anyone else in the family.

"My father wanted to raise us in America so we could have a chance to go to college," Junior said.[2]

The house Junior's family moved into was a rickety shack on Zeiss Street in Oceanside, California, a town just north of San Diego. Zeiss Street was on the east side of town—the poor side.

"My two sisters, who lived inside the house, always bragged that they had a carpet in their bedroom," Junior remembered. "But we'd say, 'So what? We have the biggest door in the whole place.'"[3]

Junior's real name is Tiaina Seau, Jr. He was named after his father. Rather than call him Tiaina, Jr., his family simply called him Junior. The name stuck.

Junior's father took a job as a custodian at a local high school. His mother, Luisa, stayed home to raise the children. Junior practiced his Samoan customs even after coming to America. In the home, he and his brothers wore wraparound skirts called lavalavas. His sisters wore floor-length dresses called muumuus. The boys did the slap dance. The girls danced the hula.

Before breakfast each day, and again after dinner, the family gathered for prayers on straw floor mats in the living room. Junior's father read from the Bible and led the singing of Samoan hymns. "Dad taught us about morals, values, and goals," Junior said. "The one question he always asked us was, . . . 'How do we protect the Seau name?'"[4]

Junior began speaking English at seven, but he could not read, write, or speak well through much of elementary school. He tried to assert himself in other ways, like fighting. When Junior was in the second grade, his older brothers began parading him around Zeiss Street, in search of older boys to fight him. Junior was forced by his brothers to fight sixth graders. "To challenge older boys and win was a big accomplishment," Junior said.[5]

Junior and his brothers were often finding trouble, and their father was quick to punish them. "There were a lot of spankings—with sticks, shoes, whatever was laying around," said Junior's older brother Savaii. "If we even thought about going to the right after dad told us to go to the left, we got our whippings."[6]

Junior's father learned discipline from his grandfather, who was chief of a village in Samoa. The neighborhood children feared Tiaina, Sr., especially the way he looked at them.

"My father has killer eyes—one goes one way, the other the other way," said Junior. "You don't know if he's looking at you when he's speaking to you, and when he's sitting to your side, one eye follows

FACT

Before each of his home games, Junior's family members and friends gather in the parking lot outside of San Diego's Jack Murphy Stadium for a big tailgate party. Junior's mother, Luisa, always wears a Charger jersey with her son's number 55 over her muumuu, and she serves up huge platters of barbecued and sweet and sour chicken, roast pork, rice, taro, and bananas. Junior's wife, Gina, calls the gathering of dozens of people "a little Samoan village."[7]

you. It's intimidating. My friends used to be so afraid of him that they'd stand in the middle of Zeiss Street and call for me to come out and play."[8]

What Junior shared most with his friends was a love of sports. He played them all, and especially enjoyed football and basketball. In sixth grade, he teamed with four boys his age—Sai Niu, Morey Paul, Kevin Hardyway, and Darrell Noble—to win the Boys Club basketball title for their age.

By seventh grade, Junior already had visions of someday playing professional sports, but he didn't just dream about it; he worked hard to achieve it. Every morning in the garage, while his brothers slept, Junior rose quietly and lifted dumbbells in front of a mirror. Every night before going to bed, he dropped to the garage floor to do hundreds of push-ups and sit-ups. Then he would go out to the backyard and do chin-ups from the limb of a maple tree.

Junior had just two things on his mind when he entered Oceanside High School as a freshman: football and fighting. On the football field, he became an instant star, playing defensive lineman and linebacker and leading the freshman team through an undefeated season. The Oceanside varsity hadn't been to the playoffs in a decade, but coach Pat Kimbrel told reporters, "Wait until next year. We

From the time he was in the seventh grade, Junior Seau worked hard to become a professional athlete. Seau continues to work hard during every NFL game.

have this freshman who is going to be a monster for the next three years."[9]

Junior was a monster on the playground as well, often picking fights. "I thought I was Mr. Macho as a freshman," he said later. "School was no part of me. I got into rumbles."[10]

After one ugly fight, Junior was suspended from school for four days. His father was furious, not because of the fighting, but because Junior would miss school. "My dad was brutal when it came to losing education," Junior said. "He didn't care that I got suspended for fighting. He wanted to know how I was going to make up all that work."[11]

At the end of Junior's freshman year in high school, his brothers had a long talk with him. Junior realized he was letting his father down. The family had moved from Samoa so the children could receive a better education, but Junior knew he was not doing his part. He decided to change his ways. He decided to take school seriously.

Junior's uncle, Wally Molifua, was a teacher at Oceanside High. Wally helped Junior with a study plan. When school started again in September, Junior went right to work, and he never stopped. He got two *B*s and the rest *A*s as a sophomore, then got straight *A*s his junior and senior years. Junior was

FACT

Junior started the Junior Seau Foundation in 1992 to promote drug and alcohol awareness, child-abuse prevention, and anti-juvenile delinquency programs. Junior donates thousands of dollars to the program each year, and speaks to children everywhere. His message is always the same. "I'm living proof," he says, "that you can make it out of the ghetto."[12]

thankful for his brothers' advice. "I consider myself lucky," he said.[13]

Junior dominated on the football field as well. All the Seau children were expected to work at after-school jobs to help the family—everyone, that is, except Junior. His father recognized his natural physical talents, and hoped his son would make his way out of the East Side through sports. "I have never worked all my life," Junior said upon graduating from high school. "[My] sister used to always complain that I wasn't doing my share. But my father told her that all my work on the football field would pay off one day."[14]

Junior's varsity football career did not begin well. At practice in the first week of his sophomore season, he crashed into a teammate and suffered a broken collarbone. He missed the first seven games of the season. After two months of watching from the sideline in frustration, Junior finally got to suit up. His first varsity game was at league rival Carlsbad High. He played middle linebacker. His Pirates allowed the game's first score, a 53-yard touchdown pass in the first quarter. In the second quarter, Junior single-handedly won the game. He stepped in front of a Carlsbad receiver, intercepted the pass, and returned it 12 yards for a touchdown. The Pirates took the lead on a two-point conversion.

Junior helped shut out Carlsbad the rest of the game.

Junior's performance a week later was even more impressive. At Oceanside's homecoming game against Torrey Pines High, the Pirates' quarterback went down with an injury in the second quarter. Junior stepped in to play quarterback, even though he had never done so before. He scored all 3 touchdowns to lead the Pirates to an 18–13 victory.

Oceanside finished the season with a 5–5 record, and the Pirates missed the playoffs for the tenth straight season, but Junior simply traded in his helmet and pads for a basketball uniform. He wanted to be a two-sport star.

Unlike the school's football team, the basketball team had a winning reputation. It had won the San Diego county 2-A title twice in the previous three years. Only two starters returned, though, and Junior was immediately named a starter. At six foot three, he displayed a fierce desire to grab rebounds with a feathery shooting touch. By the twentieth game of the season, Junior was the team's leading scorer, and the Pirates were headed for the playoffs.

Junior saved his best for the playoffs. In the semifinal, with his parents watching from the stands, Junior took control of the game. His fiery spirit intimidated Chula Vista High into shooting less than 30 percent from the field. Yet with five minutes left in the game, Chula Vista led, 33–31, and Junior was angry. Oceanside coach Bill Christopher benched Junior and gave him a harsh talking-to. "It's been the same all season," the coach said afterward. "Junior's such a fierce competitor and so young. He gets upset. When he gets upset, his eyes get a fuzz in them like the fuzz on the TV when it goes off late at night."[15]

Junior calmed down and was sent back into the game with four minutes left. The Pirates trailed by four points. Junior grabbed an offensive rebound, got fouled, and made both free throws. Then he forced the Spartans to commit a turnover. At the offensive end, he grabbed another rebound, and put it back up and in. Tie game.

Junior scored again to give the Pirates a two-point lead, and soon the Spartans were down to their final chance. With one second left, Chula Vista forward George Brynd put up a shot from inside the key. Junior swatted it out of bounds. Oceanside held on for a 42–40 win, and a moment later, Junior was in the stands, holding onto his parents, smiling and hugging them.

In the county 2-A title game four nights later, at the San Diego Sports Arena, Oceanside was locked in a defensive struggle with Mission Bay High. The

Pirates led by two points at the half, 23–21. Junior told his team in the locker room to tighten the defense another notch. The Pirates listened. With Junior clogging the middle, Mission Bay was held to just one basket in the third quarter. Oceanside won the county championship in a rout, 63–40. Junior made 6 of 8 baskets from the field and finished with 14 points. Afterward, Junior was quick to compliment others. "A lot of people said we didn't have enough talent to win the CIF," he said. "But they forgot about one thing. They overlooked our coaching."[16]

Junior had to get used to losing all over again when football season began. As frustrating as his sophomore year was, his junior season was worse. The team did not have a quarterback, and Junior was pressed into playing the position, even though he was not very good at throwing the ball. He was the best athlete on the team, however, so his coaches asked for his help. Junior did the best he could. He also played middle linebacker.

The Pirates won three games all year. In a two-week stretch that typified the season, they shut out Carlsbad, 7–0, as Junior led a defense that forced 6 turnovers; then they lost to San Dieguito, 7–6, despite Junior's 67-yard touchdown run in the first quarter.

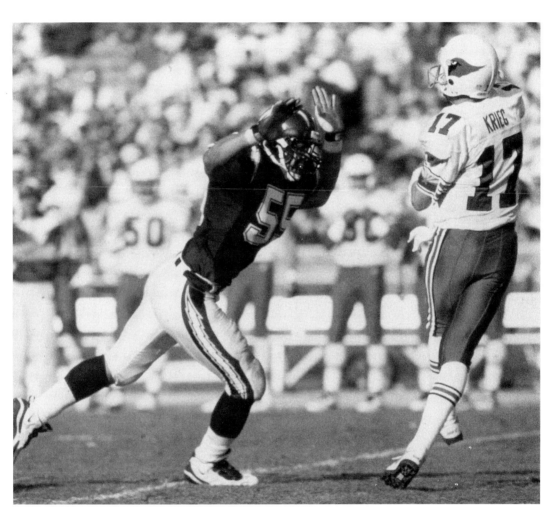

Part of Seau's job is to make life miserable for opposing quarterbacks. When he was in high school, though, sometimes he had to play quarterback himself.

FACT

Junior Seau concentrated mainly on football and basketball at Oceanside High School because they are his favorite sports. When Junior was a senior, though, the school track coach convinced him to join the track team. He competed in the shot put and discus. His technique was not polished, but by sheer strength alone, he finished second in the shot put in the county championships.

Back on the basketball court, Junior was his team's only returning starter from the previous year. He was enough. The Pirates jumped out to a 10–1 record, largely on Seau's scoring and defense. He scored 20 points in a win over Mt. Carmel, and no one else scored in double figures. He scored 17 points in a victory over Vista, half his team's points, and helped hold Vista to a single basket in the decisive fourth quarter. When teams began to triple-team Seau, he learned to dish the ball off. "He's passing the ball more and including his teammates," Coach Christopher said as the Pirates improved to 17–3. "He's making people around him play better, and that's where you want your best player."[17]

Junior was excelling on the basketball court, the football field, and in the classroom, but he still had one character flaw that needed work. He was a hothead. He sometimes lost control of his emotions, and his teammates suffered for it. In a game against city rival El Camino, Junior overheated. Two minutes into the contest, a shoving match between two players erupted into a wide-open brawl as players threw punches and fans poured from the stands to join the melee. It took twenty minutes to clear the floor and resume play. By now, Junior was boiling mad. In the second period, El Camino's Edmund

Johnson left his feet for a layup. Junior lowered his shoulders and drilled Johnson, sending him crashing to the floor. Seau was immediately ejected from the game. "That was the most flagrant technical foul I've ever seen in ten years," said referee Rod Miller.[18] Without Seau, the Pirates lost a close game.

At practice the next day, Coach Christopher told Junior he was benched for a game. Junior accepted the punishment. The coach also told Junior to go back to El Camino High to apologize. Junior agreed. The El Camino players appreciated his apology.

The Pirates reached the 2-A county championship game for the third straight year, but this time they lost. Perhaps fittingly, they lost to El Camino.

"At El Camino, I messed up," Junior admitted a month later. "I knew I did something bad. I couldn't sleep at night, wondering what people thought of me, if they thought I was a jerk. I'm learning, not just to be a better basketball player, but a better person."[19]

Chapter 3

High School All-American

High school was providing Junior with many lessons. One he had grown tired of learning was how to lose on a football field. Junior had stopped growing at six feet three inches, and he knew pro basketball was unlikely. That left football, but if his team didn't win, who would see him play? His family couldn't afford to send him to college. He needed to earn a college scholarship. He had been receiving letters from college scouts, but really, how interested were they in a linebacker who played on a losing team? Junior desperately wanted his football team to win his senior year.

The first day of practice, twelve players showed up. The team had a new coach—a man named Roy Scaffidi. Winning appeared hopeless.

Junior figured he would play quarterback on offense and safety on defense. Coach Scaffidi had other ideas. He said Junior would be more valuable as an outside linebacker and wide receiver. Seau was shocked.

"What [was] this dude doing?" he said. "I'd never played wide receiver. I thought it was ridiculous."[1]

Junior's father tried to persuade his son to transfer to another school, perhaps El Camino or Vista. Junior nearly did. Out of loyalty, he stayed. "The school had been there for me," he said later. "Teachers and boosters had been good to me. I couldn't leave."[2]

Scaffidi convinced six more boys on campus to join the team, increasing the total to eighteen.

In the season opener at mighty Vista, the Pirates trailed just 7–0 at the half, before being overwhelmed by Vista's depth. Junior walked off the field inspired. "The Pirates are back," he said. "If we can play Vista that tough, we're going to do it."[3]

Junior was right. With an efficient passing game led by quarterback Rocky Aukuso and the county's new great receiver—Junior Seau—the Pirates scored three touchdowns or more in six of their next seven games. Also, with Seau leading the defense, the Pirates allowed just four touchdowns *total* in those seven games. They won all seven.

The seventh victory came at heated crosstown rival El Camino, and it was the sweetest of all. With five minutes left in the third quarter, El Camino was clinging to a 7–6 lead. Oceanside embarked on a drive from its own 37. Aukuso looked to his main target—Seau. Junior entered the game as the county's second-leading receiver, and he showed why on the drive. First, he split two defenders to haul in a pass for 17 yards. Next, he skied to catch a high throw for 10 more. Then, he made a one-handed grab across the middle for 11 more. Finally, he caught a slant-in and bowled over two defenders for 14 yards more. The Pirates scored on the next play on an 8-yard run by Sai Niu.

On defense, Junior ended El Camino's next drive with a sack. Then, he clinched the victory by pulling in a one-yard pass for a touchdown.

On the field after the game, Junior was surrounded by family and friends. In his right hand, he held his helmet. In his left hand was a wad of bills, gifts from family members. Since Junior did not have an after-school job, his family members each paid him five dollars each time the Pirates won. "That's the minimum," he told reporters. "The more I do, the more I get."[4]

As Coach Scaffidi watched Junior walk off the field from a distance, he pointed and said, "You won't see many like him. They don't come along very often."[5]

By now, Junior was being flooded with recruiting letters and phone calls. College coaches even knew the number of the pay phone in the school cafeteria. Junior realized that he could attend the university of his choice, and it was sometimes difficult to focus on the high school season. When that happened, he only had to remind himself of the frustrations he felt—the frustration of missing most of his sophomore year with an injury, and the frustration of losing so many games as a junior. This year there was no frustration. For the first time in twelve years, Oceanside High was going to the football playoffs.

Junior kept charging in the playoffs. In the first round, he led the Pirates to a 43–0 rout of Hoover High. Junior scored the game's first touchdown on a 43-yard reception, then came back with another score from 17 yards out. He finished with six receptions for 134 yards, and had two sacks and an interception on defense.

In the semifinal round against La Jolla High, the Pirates were locked in a 14–14 tie when Junior took control. First, he caught a 13-yard touchdown pass to give his team the lead. Then, he sacked the quarterback, caused a fumble, and recovered the ball at the La Jolla 20-yard line. Two plays later, the Pirates led, 27–14. They went on to win, 35–27, to advance to San Diego's Jack Murphy Stadium and the 2-A championship. They would meet powerful Lincoln High, for a game in which Seau was "worth the price of admission alone," according to coach Scaffidi.[6]

Oceanside's eighteen players were outmatched in the title game, even with Seau. Lincoln won 41–7, but the loss did not dampen the spirits of Junior Seau. He had thrilled his school by leading a small group of players farther than anyone figured they could go, and he had proved his value on the football field. He was named to the Parade High School All-America Team at a special position created for the first time, just for him—Athlete.

Junior closed out his high school athletic career with another exciting basketball season, though it didn't begin that way. Bill Christopher stepped down as coach, and assistant Don Montamble took over. Then, with Seau still playing football, the team opened the season with five straight losses.

When Junior joined the team, the starting lineup included Sai Niu, Morey Paul, Kevin Hardyway, and Darrell Noble, the same lineup that had won the Boys Club title when they were sixth graders. The Pirates immediately made a pact: Start winning and get back to the title game at the Sports Arena—and

Seau is not only big and strong, he is also extremely coordinated. Because of his versatility, Seau was named a Parade All-American in high school, and his position was listed simply as "Athlete."

that's just what they did, with Junior leading the way. On a team featuring defense and a slow-tempo offense, Seau was the county's second-leading scorer at 22.3 points per game.

It was not always fun and games on the court, however. College football recruiters hounded Junior before and after games, and sometimes even during them. It got so crazy that Junior often slipped out of a side door as soon as the game ended, not even joining his teammates in the locker room.

"He was a man among boys," USC football coach Larry Smith said after watching Junior play a basketball game. "He was jumping over 'em, around 'em, and through 'em. You don't see a football player dominate a basketball court like that very often. [I think he's one of the future superstars of college football."[7]]

Coach Smith admired Seau so much that he offered him a four-year college scholarship on the spot. Junior admired USC so much that he accepted. The recruiting chaos would finally be over.

Now Junior could concentrate on the basketball playoffs. The Pirates blew past three opponents to reach the 2-A championship game. Their opponent: crosstown rival El Camino High.

Unlike the previous year, when El Camino blew out the Pirates, this game was close. Junior was almost perfect from the field, and to no one's surprise, he led all scorers. The game was tied 51–51, with thirty-four seconds left when Seau took a pass in the lane, turned, and hit a soft six-foot jumper. It was the winning basket. Junior wound up making 10 of 11 shots from the field, to finish with 23 points.

Four months earlier, Junior had been named San Diego County's football Player of the Year. Now, he became the first athlete ever to be named county football *and* basketball player of the year in the same school year. One Los Angeles-area coach even called him "the best player I've seen all year."[8]

By now, Junior had become a local celebrity. His number eleven football jersey was retired. He made numerous speaking appearances at elementary schools, junior highs, and social service clubs. After he spoke to sixth graders at South Oceanside Elementary, the principal, Bill Wagner, said, "He had 'em spellbound." A teacher, Sharon Cowman, said, "I can't think of a better guy to help kids."[9]

Junior said he simply wanted to give something back to the Oceanside residents who cheered for him through high school. "I enjoy going into the community teaching them something I learned," he said.[10]

One thing Junior failed to learn was how to take the Scholastic Aptitude Test (SAT). He did not prepare

Seau is a great player on the field and a good person off the field. Even when he was in high school, he would give inspirational speeches to younger kids.

well for it, and he scored 690—ten points short of the minimum requirement to be eligible for college athletics as a freshman. Even though Junior finished high school with a 3.7 grade point average, he would be forced to sit his first year at USC. He could not even practice with the team.

Junior was shocked at first. "I don't know what happened," he said. "When I took the test, I thought I did well enough. I can't understand it."[11]

Later, he admitted that he had not studied enough. "I was overconfident . . . going into the test," he said. "I had not prepared for it. I took it easy. I didn't work at the test and that is something I'm always going to regret."[12]

As the summer drew nearer, Junior began to feel guilty. He thought he had shamed the Seau family name. "Everything I'd worked for, everything my family had stood for was gone," he says now. "I was labeled a dumb jock. . . . I found out who my true friends were. Nobody stuck up for me—not our relatives, best friends or neighbors. There's a lot of jealousy among Samoans, not wanting others to get ahead in life, and my parents got an earful at church: 'We told you he was never going to make it.'"[13]

Chapter 4

College Career

Junior sat in his dormitory room at USC on fall afternoons listening to the sounds of football practice down below. He shut his bedroom window, but still he could hear the sounds.

"I'd hear everything," he remembered. "I'd hear the grunts, the hitting, the people yelling and the horns blowing. All the things that would make me wish I was out there. I could visualize everyone having a good time."[1]

Junior suffered in his freshman year. The college classroom work was easy enough. So was the homework. After all, Junior had developed good study habits in high school. It was painful not to be allowed to practice or play football, however.

Junior took out his frustration in the weight room. He lifted gigantic amounts of weight, and in nine months he added twenty-five pounds of muscle to his six-foot-three-inch frame. He now weighed 240 pounds. He got faster, too. He ran so many wind sprints that he became one of the fastest players on the team. He discovered this by winning the annual USC Superman contest—a competition of running and weight-lifting events. It was his one chance to compete against his fellow football players. No freshman had ever won the Superman contest before.

Junior also took out his frustration by fighting. Twice he broke his own hand punching somebody. "I was going out and being Mr. Macho Man, trying to prove myself, and not channeling my energy into something positive," he admitted later. "I was making the situation worse. I had all that energy and I didn't know where to put it."[2]

One time, five of Junior's high school friends came to Los Angeles to visit him. Junior took his friends to a party where USC football players were gathered. At one point during the party, Junior's friends, who were nearly as big as Junior, got into a disagreement with some of the football players. Junior had to step into the middle. "I told my friends to back off because this is my home now and I have to live with these people," Junior recalled.[3]

Junior Seau chose to play college football at the University of Southern California, but he had to sit out his freshman year.

Junior's big friends turned on him, accusing him of sticking up for his teammates over them. A fight broke out. Junior clobbered a few people, but not without breaking his own hand. He convinced his friends to go back to Oceanside. Two weeks later, Junior showed up at his old high school to watch a basketball game. When he was asked about the cast on his hand, all Junior said was, "It's a big city up there."[4]

Junior's sophomore year promised to be different. He would finally get to play football. USC had a roster of stars, but Junior made up his mind that he would play. "I'm determined to start the first game," he said. "No hiding about it. I will prove myself in practice. I'm not going to wait. I've waited enough."[5]

Junior came out roaring. In the first week of fall practice, he stunned the coaches with his ferocious play at linebacker. "From what I've seen so far . . . ," said head coach Larry Smith, "he's like a caged tiger. He's a smart football player, and he's intense. I think he'll be a starter."[6]

Then disaster struck. The team was running a full-line drill, in which players take turns running through two rows of players holding pads. As Junior ran through the lines, his ankle gave out. He collapsed to the ground, screaming in pain. He was helped into the locker room, where a team doctor found that Junior had suffered severely sprained ligaments. He would miss the last three weeks of fall practice, and the first three games of the season. Once again, Junior would have to sit.

When the big day finally arrived, when Junior finally got to play in his first college game, he truly was like a "caged tiger." It had been thirteen months since he came to USC to play football, thirteen months of waiting. The date was September 24, 1988. The site was the Los Angeles Memorial Coliseum. The opponents were the Oklahoma Sooners.

Junior did not start the game. He stood on the sideline, dressed in jersey number fifty-five, his helmet on his head, and anxiously waited. At last, with eight minutes to go in the first half, Coach Smith came over. He looked up at Junior and said, "Go in and steam them."[7]

Seau ran onto the field with his defensive mates. Three plays later, Oklahoma punted. USC scored a touchdown to take a 10–0 lead, and now it was Junior's turn again to try to stop the Sooners. On first down at the 15-yard line, Junior lined up as an outside linebacker. He was about to make the biggest defensive play of the game. Sooners quarterback Jamelle Holieway took the snap and

Seau first saw action as a sophomore at USC, and it did not take him long to make his presence felt. In his first game, he made a great play to force a fumble.

started to backpedal. Holieway was a Heisman Trophy candidate because he could run or pass with great skill. Junior didn't know if this play was an option run or a pass. All he saw was Holieway's jersey number—4—in front of him. He ran straight for it.

The play was a pass. Holieway cocked his arm to throw, but before he could get the pass off, Seau slammed into him from the blind side. The hit was so fierce that it jarred the ball loose. USC nose guard Don Gibson recovered it at the 6-yard line. One play later, tailback Aaron Emanuel scored to give USC a 17–0 lead. The Trojans would win, 23–7.

In the locker room afterward, Junior told reporters he almost blew the play. "I had outside containment, but I . . . broke inside. That could have been bad. . . . I think I didn't do my job right," he said.[8]

USC defensive coordinator Chris Allen was amused to learn Junior felt he had made a mistake. "He didn't," the coach said. "But he doesn't know it yet. Junior's still learning. That was a great instinctive play."[9]

Seau was not happy about the rest of his sophomore season. He took too many risks on the field, and sometimes he got burned. "I didn't have any techniques," he said after the season. "All I wanted to do was bang and bang and more bang. I was wild.

I thought the only way I'd make first string was to gamble, and I was failing when I gambled."[10]

Junior's season hit a low point the last game of the year against rival UCLA and quarterback Troy Aikman. Before the game, Junior predicted, "I'm going to pressure Aikman into having a bad day by giving him the worst nightmare of his lifetime."[11] Seau came out wildly on defense, though, not staying in his linebacker area, and his gambles cost the Trojans big yardage. Junior was pulled from the field by Coach Smith after just five plays.

Seau learned a valuable lesson that day. He learned that great talent is worthless if it is not harnessed. He learned the importance of discipline and team play.

Junior Seau was on a mission now. He was determined to restore pride and honor to the family name. His junior year would be great. There would be no wild play. He would do what the coaches told him. He studied game film through the summer and talked with coaches every day. He learned how to play the linebacker position. As the season approached, it was clear that he was focused. "People think I lost only one year because of [being ineligible]," he said. "But I lost two. All I did last year was learn what I missed [my first year]. . . . I'm finally getting a grip on what I'm supposed to be doing."[12]

Then disaster struck again. In the team's first fall practice, in the same full-line drill in which he was injured a year earlier, Junior accidentally jammed his finger into a pad. His finger snapped. It was broken. "The end of my finger was hanging down," he said. "I was in so much pain."[13]

After looking at his finger for a minute, Junior made a decision. He would not complain about it. Yes, it was broken. Yes, the coaches could see his pain. He decided that he still was not going to miss any part of his junior season, not even one day of practice. "It was hard for me to look at my finger and say I'm going to play," Junior recalled. "Mentally, it almost destroyed me. But I had to gut it out or I was afraid I'd have to sit out the rest of my life. How many more chances were they going to give me? The years were going by."[14]

Junior was in the trainer's room each day, before and after practice. He took painkillers. He refused surgery. He waited for the season to start.

On a warm September afternoon in Los Angeles, Junior showed a national television audience how great he could be. Playing against powerful Ohio State, Junior was overwhelming. He registered 2 sacks. He threw running backs for losses 4 times. He batted down 4 passes. He led USC to victory, 42–3. Afterward, Junior did not brag to reporters about his performance. "I'm still learning," he said humbly. "I have a long way to go."[15] Junior was right.

In a heated Pac 10 Conference game against Cal three weeks later, he reverted to his old bullying style. Once again, it got him in trouble. USC's defense was embarrassing Cal, and the Trojans had just intercepted a pass in the end zone. A shoving match broke out. Seau jumped in to help teammate Scott Ross. Seau and Cal center Steve Gordon threw punches and were ejected. The Trojans won the game, 31–15, but Coach Smith was not pleased. "Seau is not a dirty player, but he's got to learn to control his emotions," he said. Junior agreed. "Frustrations broke out," he said. "Getting ejected wasn't something I looked for. It was stupid."[16]

Against Stanford two weeks later, USC led 13–0, but Stanford appeared set to score. It was second down and a yard to go at the 8-yard line when Seau took matters into his own hands. He hit Tommy Vardell behind the line and dropped him for a one-yard loss. He batted down Steve Smith's pass on third down. He blitzed Smith on fourth down and forced an errant throw. USC turned around and marched 91 yards for a clinching touchdown.

At Arizona in mid-November, USC needed a victory to win the Pac 10 Conference and gain a berth in the Rose Bowl, but Arizona had not lost on its home field all season. Junior Seau didn't care. He led a defensive charge that kept the Wildcats out of the end zone all day, and USC won with ease, 24–3. Seau chased down running backs and receivers with his speed, and disrupted pass plays with his blitz. Arizona quarterback Ronald Veal was so nervous about Seau that he would peek around for Seau while calling signals at the line. "Junior Seau," said Arizona coach Dick Tomey afterward, "is the best player I have ever been on the field against as a coach." Reporters asked Tomey about other players, but Tomey wanted to talk only about Seau. "What a force he is," said the coach. "I have never seen such a dominant player before. He plays with more intensity and more spirit than whole teams put together."[17]

USC's defense finished third in the nation in yards allowed and points allowed. The last four games of the season, with Seau fully charged, the Trojans gave up just 19 points total. Junior led the team in tackles and finished the season with an amazing 19 sacks. To no one's surprise, he was named Pac 10 Conference Defensive Player of the Year.

There was still one college game to play, though—the Rose Bowl against Michigan. Junior was ready. "I'm the aggressor," he said. "I want to play in Michigan's backfield."[18]

In the warmth of a January sun in Pasadena, California, Junior Seau dominated once again. Early in the second quarter of a scoreless game, USC's defense forced Michigan to punt. Trojans' lineman Dan Owens rushed in with Seau, and together they blocked the punt. Seau scooped up the ball at the 35-yard line and took off. He ran 24 yards before getting tackled at the 11. Two plays later, USC scored a touchdown. Michigan threatened to tie it late in the half when it reached the 5-yard line, but Seau sacked quarterback Michael Taylor to thwart the drive.

Michigan running back Leroy Hoard reached the end zone late in the third quarter to tie the score, 10–10. Michigan would not score again. USC pulled out the win on a last-minute touchdown when half-back Ricky Ervins galloped in from 14 yards out. USC won, 17–10.

Junior had such an impressive season, capped by another great performance, that television announcer and former NFL coach Dick Vermeil called him "the Lawrence Taylor of college football."[19] Junior appreciated the compliment, but what he really

In his junior year at USC, Seau was incredible. He was the brightest star on a team that went on to win the Rose Bowl.

wanted to know was how he compared to the great LT at a higher level.

After the Rose Bowl, Junior made an announcement: He was skipping his senior year at USC. He was going to make himself eligible for the NFL draft. Junior was ready to turn pro.

Chapter 5

Playoff Contenders

Junior Seau grew up rooting for the San Diego Chargers. He dreamed of someday playing linebacker for them. On April 22, 1990, his dream came true. With the fifth overall pick in the NFL draft, the Chargers selected Junior.

Seau had been in San Diego two weeks earlier for a brief workout. It is customary for NFL teams to conduct individual workouts with college players in the weeks before the draft. The Chargers knew Seau could blitz the quarterback, stop running backs in their tracks, and chase ball-carriers sideline to sideline. Still, they wanted to know about his pass coverage ability, so Junior went one-on-one against linebackers coach Mike Haluchak. Junior was told to come up and bump and run. At the snap, Junior belted Haluchak, who ricocheted sideways, and

FACT
Top five NFL draft picks (1990):

Number	Name	Position	Team
1	Jeff George	Quarterback	Indianapolis Colts
2	Blair Thomas	Running back	New York Jets
3	Cortez Kennedy	Defensive lineman	Seattle Seahawks
4	Keith McCants	Linebacker	Tampa Bay Buccaneers
5	Junior Seau	Linebacker	San Diego Chargers

suffered a pulled hamstring. That was the end of the drill, and the end of questions about Seau. "I didn't mean to hurt the guy," Junior said.[1]

The Chargers were stunned that Junior was still available after the first four picks of the draft. When it was San Diego's turn to pick fifth, general manager Bobby Beathard didn't hesitate. He called out Seau's name ten seconds later. "Junior Seau is the guy we wanted if he got that far," said Beathard.

Junior Seau left USC after his junior year. The Chargers then made him the fifth player selected in the 1990 NFL draft.

"We didn't even wait for a phone call from another team looking to trade. We said, 'Send his name up.'"[2]

Beathard had joined the Chargers three months earlier. He had a reputation for building champions. He designed the Kansas City Chiefs team that reached the first Super Bowl in 1967. He built the Miami Dolphins into a powerhouse that played in two Super Bowls in the early 1970s, and he put together the Washington Redskins teams that played in three Super Bowls in the 1980s. Beathard was widely considered the best talent evaluator in football, and his first move with the Chargers was drafting Junior Seau.

The hundreds of Chargers fans who watched the draft on a big TV screen at Jack Murphy Stadium cheered wildly when Seau's name was announced. An hour later, Junior arrived in San Diego for his first professional press conference. "I'm thrilled," he told reporters. "It's one of those sweet stories you hear about."[3]

Preseason practice started in July, but before Junior could suit up, he had to sign a contract. That proved to be a difficult task. Tampa Bay linebacker Keith McCants, the No. 4 pick, had signed a four-year deal for $1.2 million a year. Junior's agent, Steve Feldman, insisted that Junior was worth as much as McCants. The Chargers disagreed, so Junior sat out. He didn't really want to sit around again, waiting to play football. He had done plenty of that already—but his agent insisted.

Junior missed all of training camp. Then he missed the first three preseason games. Finally, with one preseason game left, Junior and the Chargers agreed to a contract. It was less than McCants's deal, but Junior still had become a millionaire. He immediately bought his parents a new house.

San Diego's final preseason game was in a stadium familiar to Junior. It was at the Los Angeles Memorial Coliseum, where USC plays its home games. Instead of lining up against a Pac 10 opponent, however, Junior would play against the Raiders. He didn't play for long. On the first play of the game, Raiders guard Steve Wisniewski thumped Seau in the chest. Wisniewski has a reputation for making opponents lose their cool. Against Seau, it worked. On the second play, Wisniewski blocked Seau again. After the whistle blew, Junior reached back and punched Wisniewski in the stomach. The referee saw it. Junior was ejected.

Junior's one flaw was that he was still a hothead. He would have to learn to control such behavior in the NFL. Still, he was so talented that he earned a starting role as an outside linebacker.

San Diego's season opener was at Dallas. Junior played well, making 4 tackles, and assisting on 3 others. The Chargers were tied with five minutes left in the game, 14–14, when coach Dan Henning mysteriously called for a fake punt. It didn't work. The Cowboys took possession near midfield, and then Seau committed a costly penalty. Dallas quarterback Troy Aikman completed a pass on the left side to receiver Kelvin Martin. Seau flew in from behind and buried his helmet into Martin. The officials ruled that Martin was already down, and they flagged Seau for a late-hit. The gain plus the penalty put the ball on the 12, and Dallas kicked a field goal to win, 17–14. "Except for the penalty, I think Junior played pretty well," said Henning. "He was overanxious and hyper, and he did some things that aren't completely right. But he plays with a lot of energy and enthusiasm."[4]

Chargers coaches wondered about Seau. Could they get him to channel his energy in positive ways? Could they get him to keep his enthusiasm, yet control his temper? High school and college coaches had wondered the same things. Junior understood their concerns. "I have to be more mentally into the game," he said.[5]

Junior's competitive fire burned once again on the team's plane ride back to San Diego. Some of his teammates were laughing and joking and playing cards. Junior grew very angry. The Chargers had just lost the game. Why weren't his teammates as upset as he was? Junior sat silently and fumed. "Everybody got on the plane and started gambling," he recalled. "It didn't feel as if someone was hurt. I was hurt. I take football serious."[6]

More than one hundred family members and friends arrived at Jack Murphy Stadium the following week to see Junior play in the team's home opener against the Cincinnati Bengals. Junior's performance was just fair, though, and the team lost again, 21–16.

The Chargers had been a poor organization for a long time, with just one winning season in the last seven years. Their record was 6–10 in each of the previous two seasons. In Junior's rookie year, they did it again—another 6–10 finish.

The season ended on a high note for Junior. San Diego's last game was back at the Memorial Coliseum against the Raiders. Although the Chargers lost, 12–7, Seau finally got his first professional sack dumping quarterback Jay Schroeder in the second quarter. "This was my home turf," Junior told reporters. "This is one of those games that brought back a lot of good memories." In the locker room, Chargers defensive coordinator Ron Lynn predicted a bright future for the rookie linebacker. " . . . the progress he made without a training camp was wonderful. He's still got a ways to go, but I think he's going to be a magnificent player in this league."[7]

Junior was determined to prove his coach right. He improved his strength through an intense weight-lifting program designed by coach Ricky Lee Bryant. He studied the defensive playbook over and over again, memorizing every assignment of every defensive player for every defensive alignment. He wanted to know everything. He wanted the 1991 season to be different. He wanted the San Diego Chargers to start winning.

It didn't happen. The Chargers went 4–12. It was another nightmare season, even worse than the year before. The trouble started in Pittsburgh on opening day. The Chargers had fought back with ten fourth-quarter points to get within a touchdown, 19–13, with five minutes to go. Their offense was clicking. Even better, their defense had the Steelers pinned to a third and nineteen at the Pittsburgh 11-yard line. The offense was set to get the ball back near midfield. "I was buckled up, ready to go," said offensive lineman David Richards. "We were going to take it in, score, and get one of those wins that change everything."[8] Then, on third and long, the

FACT

Seau is considered to be one of the most athletic linebackers ever to play in the NFL. He can bench-press more than 500 pounds. He can do more than 800 squats. He has a forty-inch vertical leap. He can run a 4.55-second forty-yard dash. He can even easily outrace his two dogs, Heisman, a rottweiler, and Trojan, a golden retriever, while running his hundred-yard wind sprints.

Chargers blitzed both safeties. It was a bad coaching decision. Backup quarterback Neil O'Donnell threw a screen pass to slotback Dwight Stone in the flat. When Stone turned upfield, he was startled not to see any Chargers around him. He ran for a first down and more. He ran all the way down the field, untouched, 89 yards for a touchdown. The Chargers scored a last-second touchdown, but so what? They lost, 26–20.

The Chargers lost their first five games, beat the Raiders in Los Angeles, then lost their next three. Nothing was going right. Even when they made big plays, something would spoil them. At Denver in week four, the Chargers and Broncos were locked in a defensive struggle. With the score tied, 6–6, in the third quarter, Seau stepped up and made the play of the game. He intercepted John Elway's pass in the right flat and raced 44 yards to the end zone, but defensive lineman Burt Grossman was called for being offside. Seau's touchdown did not count. The Broncos scored three plays later to take the lead and win the game. "Bitterly disappointing," Seau said afterward.[9] At Anaheim in week seven, Seau record-ed 2 sacks and a season-high 13 tackles, but the Chargers bogged down at midfield on a last-minute drive and lost, 30–24, to the Rams.

FACT

In 1991, Junior started his own line of clothing and sports products called Say Ow Gear. Junior's company makes shirts, sweaters, sweat pants, jackets, visors, and hats with the Say Ow logo. Junior even sells his own water in grocery stores. Say Ow water is "One hundred percent spring water in a sports bottle."

The Chargers had a miserable season, but something good came out of it. Junior Seau had a breakthrough year. He confused offenses by lining up at both inside and outside linebacker and all along the defensive line. Offensive blockers didn't know where he was coming from next. He was the team's top defensive playmaker with 129 solo tackles and 7 sacks. At the end of the season, he was rewarded in a great way. He was voted into the Pro Bowl as a starting linebacker. Junior considered it the ultimate compliment because NFL players did the voting. He had clearly gained their respect.

Bobby Beathard fired coach Dan Henning at the end of the year, and replaced him with Bobby Ross, a college coach from Georgia Tech University. Not many people knew about Ross, but they trusted Beathard's wisdom. With Junior Seau now a force on defense, better days were ahead for the Chargers.

It didn't seem that way at first. The Chargers started the 1992 season just as they had the year before losing their first four games. They lost to the Kansas City Chiefs in the season opener, 24–10, even though Junior got 5 tackles, 1½ sacks, and an interception. Then they lost to the Denver Broncos, Pittsburgh Steelers, and Houston Oilers. San Diego hadn't been to the playoffs in a decade. It looked like another bleak season.

Then something amazing happened: The Chargers started winning. Led by quarterback Stan Humphries, acquired by Beathard from the Redskins before the season, and bruising running back Marion Butts, the Chargers began reaching the end zone. With Seau spearheading the defense, the Chargers became a force. They started with a 17–6 home victory over the Seattle Seahawks. Then they beat the Colts at Indianapolis, 34–14. Then they beat the Broncos at home, 24–21, and followed up with a shutout of the Colts, 26–0. Suddenly, the Chargers had a 4–4 record. What was happening?

Junior had taken control of the team. He expected to win. He *demanded* it. He felt personally responsible if the team lost. At Kansas City the following week, the Chargers lost in the final moments by one point, 14–13. On one play of the Chiefs' winning drive, quarterback Dave Krieg hit receiver Willie Davis on a short dump pass just beyond Seau's reach, and Davis broke it for a 25-yard gain. When Junior's wife, Gina, greeted him at the airport that night, she later said, "he was really quiet and close to tears. He blamed himself for the loss. He was up all night, saying, 'I should have done this. If only I had done that.' I couldn't get him to snap out of it."[10]

FACT

Like most great athletes, Junior keeps his body in good shape all year. He eats chicken and fish with rice daily. He eats several pieces of fruit a day. And he stays away from sweets. Also, he never skips a workout. "All your buddies are going out and taking trips, and there are times when you have to say no and look to a workout," he says.

FACT
NFL Defensive Players of the Year, 1990–1995

YEAR	AFC	NFC
1990	Bruce Smith, Buffalo	Charles Haley, San Francisco
1991	Cornelius Bennett, Buffalo	Reggie White, Philadelphia
1992	Junior Seau, San Diego	Chris Doleman, Minnesota
1993	Rod Woodson, Pittsburgh	Eric Allen, Philadelphia
1994	Greg Lloyd, Pittsburgh	Charles Haley, Dallas
1995	Bryce Paup, Buffalo	Reggie White, Green Bay

The next day, Seau asked permission to talk to the team, and just as he started to apologize for blowing the play, he broke down in tears. "It'll never happen again," he managed to say between sobs. Coach Ross and linebacker Gary Plummer put their arms around him to console him. Plummer said later, "He's the last person anybody would blame for a loss."[11]

The Kansas City loss was not Junior's fault, but he was right about one thing: It never happened again. The Chargers did not lose the rest of the season. San Diego won seven straight games, and some

Seau's first few years with the Chargers were losing seasons. Things started to turn around, however, in 1992. That year Seau was named NFL Defensive Player of the Year, and the Chargers made the playoffs.

Going full steam, Junior Seau looks to stop the Chiefs' Greg Hill. During a 1992 wild-card game, the Charger defense would hold Kansas City scoreless.

of the scores weren't even close. In order, they beat the Browns by one point, the Buccaneers by fifteen, the Raiders by twenty-four, the Cardinals by six, the Bengals by seventeen, the Raiders again by twenty-two, and the Seahawks by seventeen. They didn't just beat some of these teams, they blew them away. The Chargers started out 0–4 but finished 11–5, the biggest in-season turnaround in NFL history.

Junior was now being talked about as the best linebacker in football. "The guy's a buzz saw," said All-Pro defensive lineman Howie Long. "His rpm's are on redline all the time, but mentally he's under control."[12] At the end of the season, every NFL player would vote for Junior for the Pro Bowl. He would be the only unanimous choice. After that, he would be voted the NFL Defensive Player of the Year.

First, though, there was another score to settle— with the Kansas City Chiefs, in the playoffs.

The wild-card game between the Chargers and Chiefs at Jack Murphy Stadium was close for a while. Neither team scored in the first half, although San Diego got as close as the 8-yard line before fumbling. The second half was another story. Marion Butts took a handoff over left guard, juked past safety Charles Mincy, and outran cornerback Albert Lewis for a 54-yard score. After Leslie O'Neal intercepted a Kansas City pass moments later, John

Carney kicked a 34-yard field goal to increase the lead to 10–0. The Chargers closed out the scoring when Anthony Miller caught a 55-yard pass from Stan Humphries, and Steve Hendrickson bulled 5 yards into the end zone on the next play. The final score was 17–0, but really, it wasn't even that close. The Chiefs never came close to scoring, getting only as far as the San Diego 34-yard line in the first half, and never crossing midfield after that.

The San Diego defense had proved to be great—but it was not invincible. In a rainstorm in Miami the following week, the Dolphins sloshed their way to a 31–0 drubbing of the Chargers. Junior had the best game of his football career, registering an incredible 19 tackles, but Humphries threw 4 interceptions, and the defense made too many mistakes. The Chargers did not hang their heads afterward, however. They knew they would return to the playoffs. They were young, and they had Junior Seau.

Three weeks after the playoff loss, on Super Bowl Sunday, Junior purchased a full-page ad for fourteen thousand dollars in the *San Diego Union-Tribune* to thank the team's fans for their support. Among a group of photos of Chargers fans were these words: "To the Fans of San Diego. I Thank You for a Wonderful Year. Junior Seau and Family."[13]

Chapter 6

The Super Bowl and Beyond

Junior had become wildly popular. He was in constant demand for appearances, commercial tapings, interviews, and charity events. Appearing on *The Tonight Show*, he poked fun at host Jay Leno for having to wear a suit. "Don't make me slap you around," Leno joked. When Leno asked how much Junior could bench-press, Junior replied, "I can bench-press you. You're about 500 pounds, right?" Then Junior lay on his back and leg-pressed Leno a few times. The crowd roared with laughter.[1]

Yet, despite his fame, Junior remains humble. On the way home from an autograph session, the hired limousine in which he was riding got a flat tire. The driver started taking his jacket off to change it, but

Junior said, "That's OK, I've got it," jumped out, and changed the tire.[2]

"Too many athletes are living in a tiny window," Junior says. "They have no vision for themselves what they can be outside of football and what they can mean to a community. They just don't know any better. My hopes and dreams are unlimited."[3]

Despite the demands on his time, Junior still had to be a football player first. The Chargers opened the 1993 season with an 18–12 victory over the Seahawks. Afterward, Seattle offensive coordinator Larry Kennan said, "[Junior is] unlike any impact player this league has seen. He's a run 'em down linebacker."[4]

Two weeks later, in an 18–17 win over the Oilers, Seau had 7 solo tackles, 2 passes batted down, and 2 interceptions. After the second theft, Oilers quarterback Warren Moon was benched. "There's not another linebacker who does the things he does," Moon said. "It's almost like he plays possessed."[5]

Fellow Chargers linebacker Gary Plummer got straight to the point. He said, "He's the best linebacker that ever played the game. He plays inside, outside, the pass rush. He smothers receivers, stuffs backs. We call him the Tasmanian Devil. The guy is flying all over the field and making things happen."[6]

FACT

Junior has his own fan club called Team Seau. Members receive an autograph from Junior, a Say Ow visor, a packet of Seau stickers, and a newsletter. You can join by writing to: Team Seau at 2365 Northside Drive, Suite 203, San Diego, California, 92108. You can also write to Junior Seau's internet address at www.juniorseau.org.

Closing in quickly, Junior Seau prepares to deliver the hit. In 1993, Junior led the Chargers in tackles for the third consecutive year.

Junior led the Chargers in tackles for the third straight year, but the team fell short of the playoffs. They lost five close games and finished the season 8–8. It was a huge blow to Seau.

It was a difficult year in other ways as well. First, Junior's wife, Gina, went through a difficult pregnancy, and the couple's first child was born six weeks prematurely. (Today, their daughter, Sydney, is a healthy girl.) Then, Junior's little brother, Tony, was arrested for attempted murder. Tony had been involved with a gang for two years, and Junior was unable to convince him to leave it. One night, Tony smashed a house window with a baseball bat, just as another gang member fired a bullet through it, wounding a man. Tony was sentenced to ten years at the California Youth Authority. "Drugs and gangs are things I'm definitely against," Junior said. ". . . Tony did something wrong, and he knew it was wrong. This was probably the best thing for him. He could've been shot hanging around with these guys. He could've been dead."[7]

Junior came to training camp for the 1994 season with a fresh attitude. He signed a four-year contract for $16.3 million and tried to put his troubles behind him. "We're looking forward to this year," he said the first day of practice. "There was a lot of things that weighed on me last year. It was a disappointing year for all of us. We're just happy we're starting off clean. Hopefully, we can go out there and show what we can do. There is a point out there to prove."[8]

Seau and the Chargers proved plenty. They won their first six games, won the AFC Western division with an 11–5 record, and swept through the playoffs to the Super Bowl. They trailed in many games, but refused to quit. Six times they rallied from fourth-quarter deficits to win.

Opening night in Denver, a national TV audience saw how resourceful these Chargers would be in 1994. Trailing the Broncos 17–0, and again 24–6, San Diego fought back to claim the lead, 37–34. Junior was a terror all night, making 14 tackles and sacking Broncos quarterback John Elway twice. Elway is the master of comebacks, though. He moved his team on a game-winning drive to the 3-yard line with forty-three seconds left. On second down and goal, Elway rolled right. Seau ran toward him. As Elway started to throw, the ball squirted out of his hands and went straight into the air. Seau was stunned. "I saw a bright star. It was a ball twirling in the air," he said. "I just couldn't believe the ball was up there—especially coming from a guy who usually doesn't make those mistakes." Junior blasted forward and grabbed the ball out of the air. "You could have

FACT

Junior might be the most popular player in the NFL today. He receives fan mail from all over the world, from places like Australia, Europe, and Japan. He receives more than fifty thousand letters each year. It takes several giant boxes just to hold all the letters.

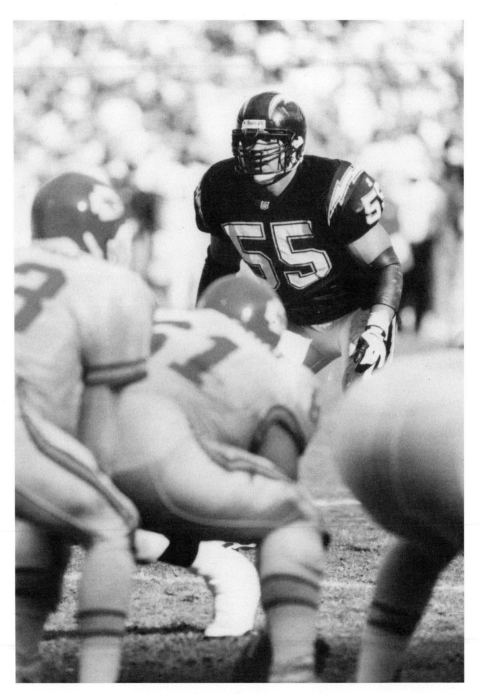

With Seau standing directly in front of the line of scrimmage, an opposing quarterback can not help feeling pressured.

chopped my hands off," he said, "and I still would have caught it."[9]

San Diego's divisional playoff game against Miami was another amazing story. The Dolphins had taken a commanding 21–6 lead at halftime. The Chargers did not quit. Seau led a defense that held the Dolphins to just 58 yards and no points in the second half. Meanwhile, the Chargers scored three times. First, defensive tackle Reuben Davis tackled running back Bernie Parmalee in the end zone for a safety. Next, bruising back Natrone Means stormed 24 yards down the sideline, carrying Dolphins cornerback J.B. Brown the final 7 yards on his back, into the end zone. Finally, with half a minute left, Stan Humphries lobbed a pass over the middle that receiver Mark Seay took 8 yards for the score. Dan Marino moved the Dolphins into field goal range in the dying seconds, but Pete Stoyanovich's 48-yarder sailed wide right, and the fans at Jack Murphy Stadium erupted.

San Diego had lost the AFC Championship Game twice in the early 1980s, but these Chargers—assembled by Bobby Beathard, coached by Bobby Ross, and led by Junior Seau—were a team of destiny. They came back from a 13–3 deficit at Pittsburgh to stun the Steelers and the football world with a 17–13 victory. Seau called it "a dream come true."[10]

As the Chargers prepared to meet the San Francisco 49ers in the Super Bowl, the city of San Diego came alive with "Chargermania." Lightning bolts appeared everywhere—in house windows, on billboards, on office buildings, and as buttons on people's clothing. It seemed that everyone was talking about the Bolts. People even painted lightning bolts on their cars. San Diego's super season came crashing to a halt in the Super Bowl, however. The 49ers routed them, 49–26, at Miami's Joe Robbie Stadium.

The 49ers were concerned about Junior Seau, so they designed a game plan simply to pass the ball over him. The plan worked. Quarterback Steve Young threw a Super Bowl-record 6 touchdown passes. Junior led his team with 11 tackles and a sack, but his performance was lost amid the fireworks by San Francisco. Still, more than a hundred thousand people turned out to greet the team as they returned to San Diego that night. An hour later, Jack Murphy Stadium was filled to capacity as the Chargers arrived to unload their football gear. Junior led several players to the field, where they stood before a microphone and thanked the fans for their amazing support.

Despite 11 tackles and 1 sack from Seau, the Chargers lost Super Bowl XXIX to the San Francisco 49ers, 49–26.

San Diego's good fortune did not continue in 1995. Natrone Means missed most of the season because of a knee injury. Stan Humphries missed several games because of a shoulder injury. Cornerback Darrien Gordon missed the entire year because of a leg injury. The Chargers still had Junior Seau, though, and that was nearly enough. The Chargers were one victory from the playoffs when they arrived at the frosty Meadowlands to play the New York Giants in the final game of the season.

As usual, San Diego rallied from a fourth-quarter deficit to win. Trailing 17–7, the Chargers scored twice to tie the game. Hundreds of New York fanatics hurled snowballs at the Chargers, and the officials nearly halted the game and declared a forfeit. With five minutes left, the Giants were poised for the go-ahead score at the Chargers' 15-yard line. Quarterback Dave Brown dropped back to pass. In came Junior on a blitz. As Brown threw, Seau drilled him from the blind side. The ball fluttered toward the goal line. Safety Shaun Gayle intercepted the pass and raced 99 yards the other way.

"Amazing," yelled television announcer Cris Collinsworth. "Junior has absolutely taken over this game." With snowballs raining down from the stands, the Chargers added a late field goal to win, 27–17. "Junior Seau is incredible," Collinsworth said. "He basically put the Chargers on his back in the second half."[11]

Junior led the team in tackles, inspiration, and leadership for the fourth straight year. Once again, he was a unanimous choice for the Pro Bowl.

Sadly, San Diego's season ended in the playoffs a week later. Even the warm January sun in Southern California couldn't help the Chargers. They lost in the first round to the surprising Indianapolis Colts. Nobody predicted success for the Colts, but quarterback Jim Harbaugh led them past the Chargers, then the Chiefs, and almost past the Steelers to the Super Bowl. The Colts had learned, watching the Chargers the previous year, that a team can win through hard work and determination. San Diego, meanwhile, set its sights on the future. With Junior anchoring the defense, San Diego's goal was not just the playoffs anymore—it was the Super Bowl.

Unfortunately, the Chargers only got worse. The team finished the 1996 season, 8–8 and out of the playoff hunt. In 1997, San Diego dropped to 4–12, one of the worst records in the league. Junior Seau, however, was one of the team's bright spots. He was selected to play in the Pro Bowl after each of those seasons.

Junior Seau is so talented that Coach Ross claims he could return punts and kickoffs. General

FACT

In May each year, Junior hosts a golf tournament at exclusive La Costa Country Club north of San Diego. Dozens of NFL stars compete in the tournament. Among those who play are Steve Young, Jerry Rice, Greg Lloyd, Cortez Kennedy, Ronnie Lott, and Lynn Swann. Junior donates all money raised through concessions and ticket sales to charity.

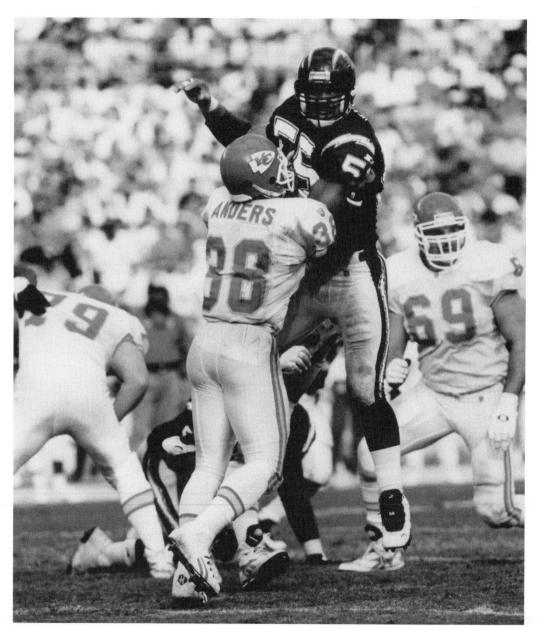

Using more than his athletic skill, Seau also prepares for games to give him an advantage. By studying films he is able to determine what the opposing team is going to do.

Manager Beathard says he could be a Pro Bowl tight end or fullback.

Junior brims with confidence about his ability. "In order to go out there and perform—and I'm not saying I'm The Man in the NFL or anything—when I'm out there, I have to believe I'm the best," he says.[12]

Junior has immense talent, but he does something else that sets him apart from ordinary pro linebackers: He studies. He learned a valuable lesson as a senior in high school, when he failed to prepare for the SAT test. He has studied and prepared himself to win ever since. "Football's a chess game—and I'm very good at chess," he says. "If you move your pawn against my bishop, I'll counter that move to beat you. Same thing on the field. I study so much film. I know exactly what teams are going to do."[13]

Junior Seau is often compared to Lawrence Taylor. He is compared to Dick Butkus. He is compared to Jack Lambert and Mike Singletary. Some people say Junior is better than all of them. Some say Junior is the best linebacker of all time. Junior won't say; he still has more football to play. "I'm on the right track," he says, "but I'm not there yet. When I'm done, I want to be known as the greatest linebacker ever. Why not want to be the best?"[14]

He may already be.

Chapter Notes

Chapter 1

1. Dick Enberg, NBC-TV telecast, January 15, 1995.

2. Michael Silver, "The Last, Best Word," *Sports Illustrated*, January 23, 1995, p. 32.

3. Jeff Savage, "Naturally, the Lottery Brought Out the Best in Everybody's Picks," *San Diego Tribune*, April 23, 1990, p. 1.

4. Samantha Stevenson, "Seau Adds His Own Dimension to Chargers' Success," *The New York Times*, January 10, 1993, p. 14.

5. Bob Trumpy, NBC-TV telecast, January 15, 1995.

6. Silver, p. 34.

7. Paul Attner, "The Young and the Gifted," *Sporting News*, October 4, 1993, pp. 34–36.

Chapter 2

1. Samantha Stevenson, "Seau Adds His Own Dimension to Chargers' Success," *The New York Times*, January 10, 1993, p. 14.

2. Tom Shanahan, "Seau Has Been a Hit as Junior," *San Diego Tribune*, November 17, 1989, p. 1.

3. Ibid.

4. Ibid.

5. Don Norcross, "He Channeled His Energies," *San Diego Tribune,* June 10, 1987, p. 1.

6. Ibid.

7. Jill Lieber, "Hard Charger," *Sports Illustrated,* September 6, 1993, p. 73.

8. Tom Shanahan, "Slow Starts, Fast Finishes are Seau's Trademarks," *San Diego Tribune,* September 15, 1990, p. 3.

9. Ibid.

10. Norcross, p. 1.

11. Ibid.

12. Jill Lieber, "Hard Charger," *Sports Illustrated,* September 6, 1993, p. 71.

13. Ibid.

14. Kevin Newberry, "Driven Seau Has Succeeded via Hard Work," *San Diego Union,* June 10, 1987, pp. C1, C6.

15. Michael Bass, "Oceanside Boys Beat Chula Vista," *San Diego Union,* February 24, 1985, p. H14.

16. Ric Bucher, "Oceanside Rips Mission Bay," *San Diego Union,* February 28, 1985, p. C4.

17. Tom Shanahan, "Seau's Best Average is in the Classroom," *San Diego Tribune,* February 11, 1986, p. 8.

18. Tom Shanahan, "Players Criticized as Fight Mars El Camino Win," *San Diego Tribune*, January 18, 1986, p. 2.

19. Shanahan, "Seau's Best Average," p. 8.

Chapter 3

1. Don Norcross, "He Channeled His Energies," *San Diego Tribune*, June 10, 1987, p. 1.

2. Ibid.

3. Ibid.

4. Don Norcross, "Pirates, Seau Cash in on Wildcats," *San Diego Tribune*, November 1, 1986, p. 2.

5. Ibid.

6. Mark Zeigler, "Hornets Put the Big Chill on Oceanside," *San Diego Union*, December 14, 1986, p. H6.

7. Kevin Newberry, "Driven Seau Has Succeeded via Hard Work," *San Diego Union*, June 10, 1987, pp. C1, C6.

8. Kevin Newberry, "Pirates' Seau Player of Year for the Boys," *San Diego Union*, March 15, 1987, p. H17.

9. Norcross, "He Channeled His Energies," p. 1.

10. Ibid.

11. Tom Shanahan, "Always Ready and Willing, Seau's Now Able to Play Football Again," *San Diego Tribune*, August 13, 1988, p. 3.

12. Mark Zeigler, "Seau Has No Interest in Labels," *San Diego Union*, December 29, 1989, pp. D1, D9.

13. Jill Lieber, "Hard Charger," *Sports Illustrated*, September 6, 1993, p.72.

Chapter 4

1. Tom Shanahan, "Always Ready and Willing, Seau's Now Able to Play Football Again," *San Diego Tribune*, August 13, 1988, p. 3.

2 Ibid.

3. Ibid.

4. Tom Shanahan, "Slow Starts, Fast Finishes are Seau's Trademarks," *San Diego Tribune*, September 15, 1990, p. 3.

5. Shanahan, "Always Ready and Willing," p. 3.

6. Bill Center, "Trojans' Team of Destiny Hopes to Re-Peete Past Glories," *San Diego Union*, August 28, 1988, p. H8.

7. Bill Center, "USC Gets Big Plays, Pads Lead," *San Diego Union*, September 25, 1988, p. H8.

8. Ibid.

9. Ibid.

10. Tom Shanahan, "Seau Has Been a Hit as Junior," *San Diego Tribune*, November 17, 1989, p. 1.

11. Ibid.

12. Bill Center, "USC's Seau Is Making Up for Lost Time," *San Diego Union*, October 6, 1989, p. D2.

13. Shanahan, "Seau Has Been a Hit," p. 1.

14. Ibid.

15. Center, "USC's Seau," p. D2.

16. Bill Center, "Trojans' 31–15 Win Not Pretty To Smith," *San Diego Union*, October 15, 1989, p. H1.

17. Bill Center, "Trojans Bowl Over Wildcats; Junior Makes Them Say, 'Ow!'" *San Diego Union*, November 12, 1989, p. H1.

18. Mark Zeigler, "Seau Has No Interest in Labels," *San Diego Union*, December 29, 1989, pp. D1, D9.

19. Ibid.

Chapter 5

1. Clark Judge, "Chargers Defense Enlists Junior Partner," *San Diego Tribune*, April 23, 1990, p. 1.

2. Jeff Savage, "Naturally, the Lottery Brought Out the Best in Everybody's Picks," *San Diego Tribune*, April 23, 1990, p. 1.

3. Judge, p. 1.

4. Ibid.

5. Ibid.

6. Samantha Stevenson, "Seau Adds His Own Dimension to Chargers' Success," *The New York Times*, January 10, 1993, p. 14.

7. Chris Clarey, "Bernstine Comeback Could Mean a Return," *San Diego Union*, December 31, 1990, p. C7.

8. Bill Center, "Breakdown in Pittsburgh," *San Diego Union*, September 2, 1991, p. E1.

9. Bill Center, "Defense is Culprit Again for Chargers," *San Diego Union*, September 23, 1991, p. D1.

10. Jill Lieber, "Hard Charger," *Sports Illustrated*, September 6, 1993, pp. 64–73.

11. Ibid.

12. Ibid.

13. Ibid.

Chapter 6

1. Don Norcross, "Say Wow: Junior Tackles TV," *San Diego Union-Tribune*, November 2, 1994, pp. D1, D8.

2. Jill Lieber, "Hard Charger," *Sports Illustrated*, September 6, 1993, pp. 64–73.

3. Ibid.

4. Paul Attner, "The Young and the Gifted," *Sporting News*, October 4, 1993, pp. 34–36.

5. Ibid.

6. Samantha Stevenson, "Seau Adds His Own Dimension to Chargers' Success," *New York Times*, January 10, 1993, p. 14.

7. Clark Judge, "Say Ouch—Seau Endured '93, Awaits His Reward," *San Diego Union-Tribune*, February 3, 1994, p. 1.

8. Kevin Kernan, "A Fresh Start—1993 Travails Just a Memory as Seau Points to Big Season," *San Diego Union-Tribune,* July 19, 1994, pp. D1, D5.

9. Kevin Kernan, "Say Wow! Seau Grabs Fumble to Seal Win," *San Diego Union-Tribune,* September 5, 1994, p. D1.

10. Kevin Kernan, "Tougher Than Steel," *San Diego Union-Tribune,* January 16, 1995, pp. D1, D13.

11. Cris Collinsworth, NBC-TV telecast, December 23, 1995.

12. Dan Dieffenbach, "Junior Seau Recharged," *Sport,* November 1995, pp. 100–102.

13. Rick Weinberg, "Junior Seau—Football's a Chess Game—And I'm Very Good at Chess," *Sport,* October 1994, pp. 22–24.

14. Dieffenbach, pp. 100–102.

Career Statistics

YEAR	TEAM	G	TACKLES			SACKS	INTS	FUM
			TACK	AST	TOTALS			
1990	Chargers	16	61	24	85	1.0	0	0
1991	Chargers	16	111	18	129	7.0	0	0
1992	Chargers	15	79	23	102	4.5	2	1
1993	Chargers	16	108	21	129	0.0	2	1
1994	Chargers	16	124	31	155	5.5	0	3
1995	Chargers	16	111	18	129	2.0	2	3
1996	Chargers	15	111	27	138	7.0	2	3
1997	Chargers	15	86	12	98	7.0	2	2
TOTALS		125	791	174	965	34.0	10	13

G=games
TACK=solo tackles
AST=assists
INTS=interceptions
FUM=fumble recoveries

Where to Write Junior Seau

Mr. Junior Seau
c/o San Diego Chargers
9449 Friars Road
San Diego, CA 92108

On the Internet at:

http://www.nfl.com/players/profile/2894.html

http://www.nfl.com/chargers

Index